SAMMY SPIDER'S
FIRST
ROSH HASHANAH

SYLVIA A. ROUSS

illustrated by
KATHERINE JANUS KAHN

KAR-BEN
PUBLISHING
www.karben.com
800-4KARBEN

To my children, Gabrielle, Shannan, and Jordan
who make all my days sweet.
—SAR

In loving memory of
Joshua and Hannah Bernhardt—
in whose house the love of God, of Judaism,
and of all people flowered. I am proud to be
part of the chain of tradition which passes it on.
—KJK

Rosh Hashanah, the Jewish New Year, comes in the fall, and begins a ten-day period called the High Holy Days. It is a time for celebration. Families and friends gather for festive meals and wish each other *Shanah Tovah*, a sweet New Year. It is also a serious time. At synagogue services, the shofar, (ram's horn) is sounded to welcome the new year. We pray for a year of happiness and peace.

Text copyright © 1996 by Sylvia A. Rouss
Illustrations copyright © 1996 by Katherine Janus Kahn

KAR-BEN PUBLISHING
A division of Lerner Publishing Group, Inc.
241 First Avenue North
Minneapolis, MN 55401 U.S.A.
1-800-4Karben

Website address: www.karben.com

Library of Congress Cataloging-in-Publication Data

Rouss, Sylvia A.
    Sammy Spider's First Rosh Hashanah / Sylvia A. Rouss ; illustrated by
Katherine Janus Kahn.
      p.   cm.
    Summary: A young spider wants to join in as he watches a family prepare
to celebrate Rosh Hashanah.
    ISBN-13: 978–0–929371–99–3 (pbk. : alk. paper)
    ISBN-10: 0–929371–99–2 (pbk. : alk. paper)
    [1. Spiders—Fiction. 2. Rosh ha-Shanah—Fiction.
3. Jews   Fiction.] I. Kahn, Katherine, ill. II. Title.
PZ7.R7622 Sao 1996
[E]—dc20   96-25665

Manufactured in the United States of America
4 5 6 7 8 9 – JR – 13 12 11 10 09 08

A BOOK OF SIZES

BIG

MIDDLE-SIZE

SMALL

Sammy Spider dangled from a silky strand of webbing near the big picture window in the Shapiros' living room.

"Look, Mother," he said, pointing with one leg. "Here comes the mail carrier with more cards for the Shapiros. Why has she been delivering so many cards this week?"

Mrs. Spider looked lovingly at Sammy. "Soon the Shapiros will celebrate Rosh Hashanah," she replied. "Those cards are from family and friends who are wishing them a *shanah tovah*, a Happy New Year."

"Will we get cards, too?" Sammy asked hopefully.

"Silly little Sammy," answered Mrs. Spider.
"Spiders don't celebrate Rosh Hashanah. Spiders
spin webs.

Which reminds me, our web is getting a little crowded.

When you were born
we lived in
a small web.

Now our web is
middle-sized,

but you grew so much
over the summer
that we need to spin a large one."

Sammy wasn't paying attention. He was hanging above the shelf watching Mr. Shapiro display the new cards. They were all different sizes.

Some were large, some were middle-sized, and some were small.

"Aren't they beautiful, Mother!" Sammy sighed.

But before Mrs. Spider could answer, Sammy
scurried across the ceiling into the Shapiros' kitchen.

Mrs. Shapiro and Josh were kneading dough and
shaping it into circles. "What are they doing now?"
he called to his mother.

"They're making round challahs for Rosh Hashanah," she answered. "Mrs. Shapiro is making a large challah for the family, a middle-sized challah for the neighbors, and Josh is making a small challah for himself."

"Can we make challah, too?" Sammy asked.

"Silly little Sammy," laughed his mother. "Spiders don't knead dough. Spiders spin webs."

The next morning Sammy woke to a chopping sound in the kitchen. Mr. Shapiro was slicing apples —

big red ones,

middle-sized
yellow ones,

and small
green ones.

Nearby Josh was filling three bowls with honey.

There was
a large bowl
for Mr. Shapiro,

a middle-sized bowl
for Mrs. Shapiro,

and a small bowl
for himself.

Mrs. Spider came over to Sammy. "Rosh Hashanah begins tonight," she explained. "At dinner the Shapiros will dip apples into honey for a sweet, new year."

"Can we dip apples, too?" asked Sammy.

"Silly little Sammy," replied Mrs. Spider. "Spiders don't dip apples. Spiders spin webs."

The next morning everyone got dressed up to go to the synagogue.

Mr. Shapiro put on his big, grey coat.

Mrs. Shapiro wore her middle-sized red coat,

and Josh put on his small blue jacket.

"I can't wait for the rabbi to blow the shofar," Josh exclaimed, as they left the house.

"Josh and his family are going to services," Mrs. Spider whispered to Sammy. "The rabbi will blow the shofar to welcome the new year."

"Can we go, too?" asked Sammy.

"Silly little Sammy," answered Mrs. Spider,
shaking her head. "Spiders don't go to synagogue.
Spiders spin webs. Come help me spin our new,
larger web."

Instead,
Sammy swung down
to the kitchen counter
and crawled toward
the bowl of apples.

In his excitement he stepped into a drop of spilled honey. All of a sudden he couldn't move. His eight little legs were stuck. He struggled to free himself.

"Help, Mother," he cried. "The honey won't let go of me!"

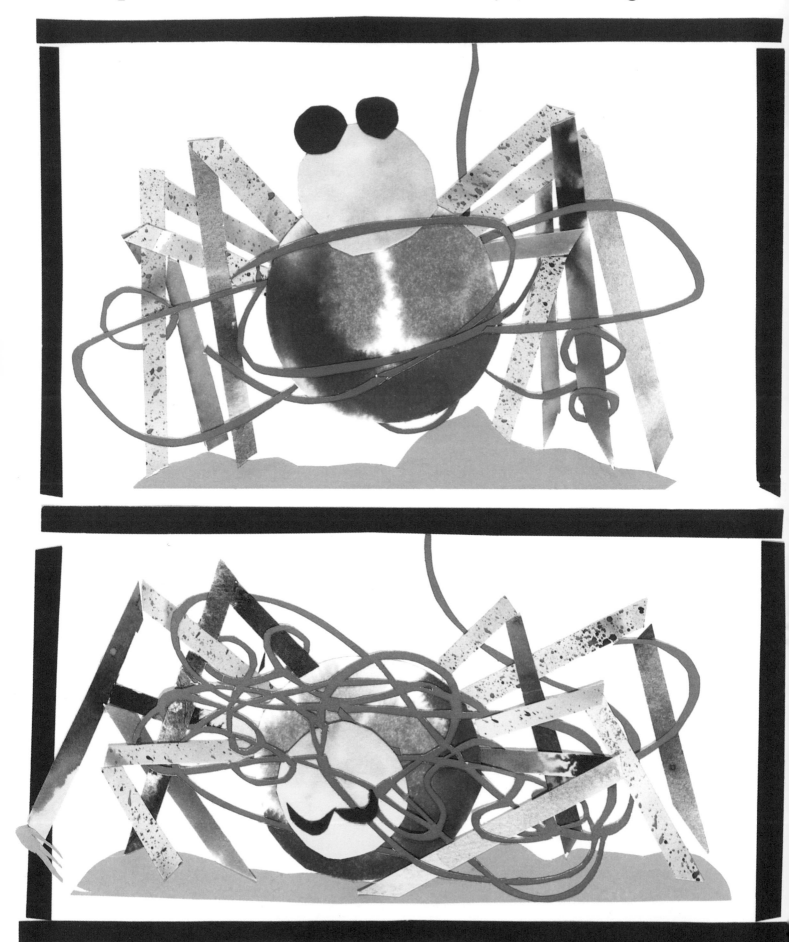

Mrs. Spider lowered herself on a strand
of webbing and tried to pull Sammy free. She
pulled and pulled until she had to catch her breath.

Sammy began to cry. As he bent his face to wipe away the tears, a drop of honey got into his mouth.

It tasted sweet.

Sammy took a little swallow,

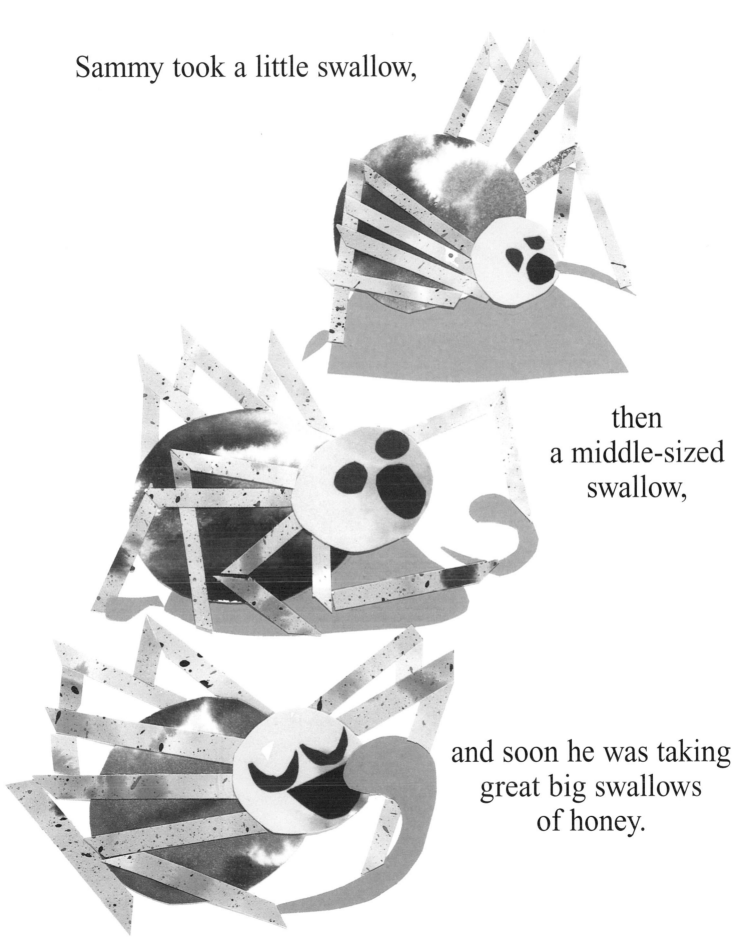

then
a middle-sized
swallow,

and soon he was taking
great big swallows
of honey.

Before he knew it, he wasn't stuck anymore.

Mrs. Spider scooped
Sammy up and held
him close.

He still felt a little sticky.
"See, Mother," he said.
"Spiders can have a sweet New Year.
All you have to do is dip me in honey!"

Mrs. Spider hugged Sammy closer. "The Shapiros
can celebrate a sweet NEW YEAR," she laughed,

"but I'm just happy to have a sweet
YOU NEAR!"

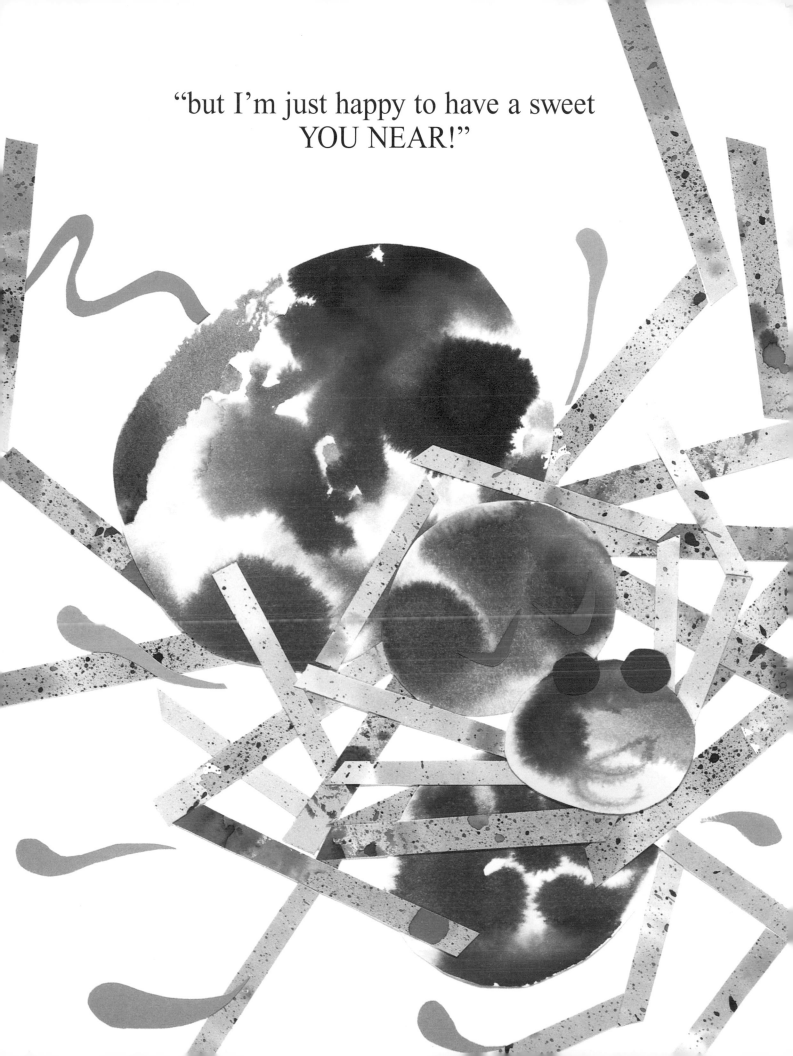

ABOUT THE AUTHOR

Sylvia A. Rouss is the award-winning author of over 20 children's books, including the popular *Sammy Spider* series. She wrote *The Littlest Pair*, which won the National Jewish Book Award and *Sammy Spider's First Trip To Israel*, which was named a Sydney Taylor Honor book by the Association of Jewish Libraries. She teaches preschool at the Stephen S. Wise Temple in Los Angeles.

ABOUT THE ILLUSTRATOR

Katherine Janus Kahn has illustrated an impressive list of more than 30 picture books, toddler board books, holiday services, and activity books for Kar-Ben. She and Sammy Spider frequently visit schools and bookstores for storytelling and chalk talks. She currently paints and sculpts in Wheaton, MD.